EPISODE #1

fast
friends

by Julia DeVillers

Printed in the United States of America

First edition, 3rd printing

ISBN 0-9678906-6-7

Visit www.limitedtoo.com

introduction

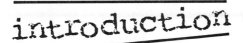

OK, so I'm sitting here in this tall chair in front of a mirror.

- ★ A makeup artist is putting lip gloss on my lips.
- ★ A hair stylist is brushing and fluffing my hair.
- ★ A fashion stylist is holding up cool outfits and asking which one is my fave.

Because I'm going to be a model! I'm here at a photo shoot!

ME!

No, I'm not a supermodel! I'm not some famous star!

I'm just me, regular Maddy Elizabeth Sparks.

What are the chances of this happening? Three days ago, I would have said:

But it turned out, it's

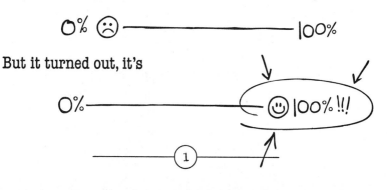

I'm still in shock.

I'm here at this photo shoot with my three new friends, Kacey, Isabel, and Claire. And it's not just the photo shoot that's getting me psyched! We're gonna get to do such incredible stuff. Like traveling to exciting places. Helping design clothes. Getting to meet celebrities. Getting backstage passes to concerts!

And I get to do all these things with Kacey, Isabel, and Claire.

Sooooo glamorous! Sooooo exciting! Sooooo unbelievable! I mean, I can't even believe it myself! Somebody pinch me! Am I dreaming?

Because just a couple days ago, I was this regular girl, doing regular stuff.

Actually, a couple days ago I was having one of the worst days of my life. ☹

But then ...

Totally out of nowhere ...

Well, let me tell you how it all happened ....

chapter 1

This Journal Belongs to:

Maddy Elizabeth Sparks

PRIVATE!

KEEP OUT!!

Zack, THIS MEANS YOU!!!!

Q: If you could have any wish come true, what would it be?

A: World peace. But my next wish would be to be a cheerleader. OK, that sounds seriously shallow next to world peace, but read on and you will totally see what I mean!!!

I am having a really bad day. More like a realllllllly bad day. Worse than the day I had toilet paper stuck to my shoe at school. Even worse than the day during math extra help class when I chewed on my pen and it broke. And there was green ink all over my mouth. And my teeth. And my nose. And I didn't know it. Until someone told me. And not just ANY someone, but RYAN MOORE!!! That's right, Ryan Moore turned around in his chair to say, "Excuse me, but did you know your face has turned green?"!!!!!!!!

(Ughhh, I don't even want to think about that)

But this day is even worse and it will affect me and my entire life!

It was so not supposed to turn out like this. Put it this way, I have taken three years of dance lessons. Invested hours of my life tapping, "plie"-ing, and hip-hopping. I have taken two years of gymnastics lessons. Invested more precious hours bouncing, twirling, and flipping. Invested my entire summer practicing cheers with my friends, getting all sweaty and hot, when we could have been in the pool.

3 years of dance +
2 years of gymnastics +
1 summer of practicing every day should =
1 place on the cheerleading team

However, for Maddy Sparks, otherwise known as ME ...

3 years of dance +
2 years of gymnastics +
The stupid way I screw everything up =
Being the only one of my friends NOT to make the cheerleading team!!!!!!!! ☹

That's right. Everybody I hang out with made the team! Everyone's who's anyone made the team! But me? Nope. Cut. Rejected. Thanks, but no thanks. I DIDN'T MAKE THE TEAM! AAAAHH!!!! I CAN'T BELIEVE I'M THE ONLY ONE OF US WHO DIDN'T MAKE THE TEAM!!!!! They only cut six girls and one of them was ME!!!!!

Not that I'm not happy for my friends, of course. I sent e-cards to them all:

Congratulations! I'll be cheering on u cheerleaders! Go, BFF, go! CU L8R. Maddy

But OK. Let's get real. It's hard to be happy when I am the ONLY one who will be TOTALLY

LEFT OUT. Alone every day after school while they're all together practicing for the competitions.

So maybe being a cheerleader isn't the ultimate most important thing in life. But I've been practicing all summer with my friends! I have the sore arms to prove it. And the practically sprained ankle from when I fell off the top of the pyramid. I earned a spot on the team! That green and white uniform should have been mine!

I tried really hard! I didn't even trip when I did my "I've got spirit, yes I do! I've got spirit how 'bout YOU?!!" routine. I smiled my best smile, I flipped my best flip, I pommed my best pom-pom!

All for nothing.

The judges obviously saw through my nothing specialness and thought, "NEXT!" Did my whole vibe just scream, "She's SO not a cheerleader!"? All of the above? Well, here I am. Maddy Sparks is a failure. A nobody. A complete zero.

Sniff.

This is seriously depressing. I hear Mom calling me. She's on a mission to cheer me up. More later. Gotta go.

What I would have guessed Mom was going to say to cheer me up:

A) It's not the end of the world, honey.
B) You tried your best and that's the best you can do.
C) If they're true friends, they'll stick by you no matter what.
D) Maybe next year.
E) All of the above.

What Mom DID say:

E) All of the above. But also ... "So what do you say we lose the men, go to the mall, and do some back-to-school shopping a little early?"

YESSSS!!!!

It took a little while to get to the mall. First, we had to "lose the men." That meant Mom had to get Dad to watch my brother Zack while we were gone. You'd think, since Zack is eight, he'd be pretty easy to watch. But he's always getting himself (or me) into trouble. So someone always has to keep a major eye on him. Then Dad had to remind her about the budget and not to go crazy and Mom had to say she knows, she knows. And I had to get dressed. Which took awhile.

I stood in my closet. I felt like I had nothing to wear! I was sick, sick, sick of my summer clothes. Good thing I'm going shopping, right?

I put on a blue T-shirt and denim shorts. Some beat-up-from-summer-camp-I-hope-Mom-will-buy-me-some-new sneakers. A choker and a blue headwrap to pull back my almost shoulder-length brown hair. I checked myself out in the mirror. I went to all this work to pull this outfit together. Could you tell? Nope. I'm still just a regular girl.

Yep, that's me, pretty regular.

I live about fifteen minutes from my favorite mall. We live in the suburbs, you know, houses, backyards, trees, regular stores you see everywhere. I live in a regular house, nothing fancy. Three bedrooms, one for my parents, one for me, one for my brother. A fenced-in yard that would be perfect for a dog.

Ask me if I have a dog. Nooooo. Ask me if I want a dog. Yes! Of course. Who wouldn't? Ask my brother Zack. He says yes! Ask my mom. She says yes! Ask my Dad.

Well, that's who wouldn't ....

Dad says no! No way. That's a big fat no. He says his job description does not include pooper scooper. Yuk!!

But I'm working on him. This morning I even brought him a glass of OJ before work. And the newspaper. Which just so happened to have a story on the front page about how a dog saved a family's life by barking when he smelled smoke.

I circled the photo of the dog with my blue gel pen and wrote, "Dogs save lives!" I laid the newspaper with that page face up.

Dad glanced at the page and said, "Thank you for the juice. And the newspaper. And for not bothering me again today about getting a dog."

Not entirely unexpected. I've been working on him for about a month with the same results. I'm hoping that sooner or later he'll crack. As Dad himself always says, "Never give up!"

So I won't.

That was early this morning, at breakfast, when life was still pretty good. Before the phone rang.

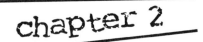

chapter 2

"It's for you, Maddy," my mom called upstairs. "Again!"

I was in my room just after breakfast, rearranging my seashell collection on my bookshelf. My bedroom walls were blue, and I was trying for an ocean effect with my blue comforter, white pillows and curtains, and my shells. My favorite thing was my bulletin board with crisscross ribbons. Stuffed on it were a bunch of pictures of me and my friends, some tickets to plays I went to, and some postcards with dogs on them. My guinea pig, Sugar, sat in her cage, chewing on some wood shavings.

I'd already had three calls from my friends before breakfast even. We were all going crazy. Because today was the day our cheerleading results were going to be posted.

It was Brittany on the phone. Brittany's mom is the cheerleading coach. We'd tried out after school yesterday and the results were supposed to be posted at the middle school at noon today. But Brittany was saying she'd snagged the list from her mom's desk. She wanted her closest, most personal friends to get the scoop before anyone else. Though if her mom knew she was on the phone spreading the news she would be in major trouble.

And Brittany was so excited!!!! Because she had made it!!! (DUH. Her mom is the coach. And a judge. I've been friends with Brittany since first grade and could have told you back then that she'd be a cheerleader. But hey, I was still happy for her.)

And then ...

"Oh, but I'm soooo sorry for you, Maddy," she'd said. "I thought you'd want to hear the news from a friend. And I thought I'd save you a trip to the school to go look at the results with everybody else standing there. So you don't look stupid or anything. Because the thing is, well, you didn't make it."

Oh.

"I know, it's a major bummer," Brittany went on. "But guess what? Jordan Cooper didn't make it either. She thinks she's all that. Ha! And she got cut. That rocks! Here's who did make it! Like everybody! Haley, Danielle, Jada, Chelsea B., Surya ..."

Buzzzzzzzzzz. My head was buzzing. It was hard to listen. I took a deep breath and then tuned back in to what she was saying.

"Caroline, Maggie, Quinn ..."

This was endless. Brittany hadn't even noticed I hadn't said a word.

"... and Shana and Amanda! I think that's everybody we know who made it," she continued. "OK, I gotta go! We have our first practice this afternoon already. I gotta call everybody! They're going to be so psyched! Bye-eee."

She hung up.

AUGH!!!!!!!!!!!!

AUGH!!!!!!!!!!!

AUGH!!!!!!!!!!!!!

I didn't make it. And all my friends did! All of them!

I was in a seriously depressed mode all morning. I sent off that e-mail to my friends and then refused to answer the phone. I just hung out in my room with my guinea pig, Sugar. Lying on my bed on my blue tie-dye pillows, I turned up my headphones and tried to tune out the world.

It just seemed like my life was spinning out of control. Things used to be so easy when I was a kid.

Now everything was changing. My friends were obsessed with making cheerleading. "We have to establish ourselves," said Brittany. We were going to a new school this year. They had put up a new building and were combining two schools. New bus, new teachers, new lockers, new people in school ... new everything. Yikes!

And then there was the worst thing of all. Even worse than cheerleading. At the beginning of the summer, Taylor moved. Not just to a new house. To a new state.

Taylor, my BFF since kindergarten. She is like my sister. I mean it.

I remember when I first met her. It was the first day of kindergarten. Back then, I had super-long hair. My mom had French-braided it for me so I could be like Rapunzel on the first day of school. I was sitting in my little wood chair, listening to Mrs. McCafferty tell the class how to do our arts and craft project. And then a girl with red hair at my table hissed.

"You cut that out, boy with the red shirt! Or I'm telling Mrs. McCafferty!"

I turned around to see a boy sitting behind me looking guilty. He had a bottle of glue in his hand. The red-headed girl was pointing at him and giving him a dirty look.

"That boy with the red shirt was about to glue your braids to your chair!" she whispered to me. She glared at him again. "Don't be mean to my friend or you'll be sorry!" she said to him. And then she smiled at me. And we've been best best best friends ever since.

And we are going to stay BFF. Forever. I mean it. I don't even care if she lives in California now. Like A GAZILLION MILES away!

So anyway. Without Taylor, it's so not the same. I mean, I've still got friends. But things have been changing lately. Brittany's been getting more, well, Brittany-like. Everybody's been WAY into whatever Brittany thinks and whatever Brittany wants to do. I knew my friends were all talking behind my back right now. I could imagine what they were saying:

Danielle: "Poor Maddy didn't make the team."
Haley: "I wonder what she screwed up."
Brittany: "My mother said she was way bad. So she'd bring down the team, anyway. I hope I'm voted captain! Come on, let's go practice!"

But Taylor wouldn't have talked about me behind my back. Even if she had made cheerleading and I hadn't. I could always count on Taylor to be there for me no matter what.

Except she can't be now. In person, anyway. Her father got transferred to Los Angeles in May. It was so all of a sudden. She was here. And now she's gone. Sometimes I still can't believe she isn't here in Columbus, Ohio, anymore.

So anyway. That's why I really, really wanted to make cheerleading. It would have given me something to focus on. I could have made some new friends on the team. And, I would have known where I fit in at the new school. I'd have known who to sit with at lunch. It would have given me an identity. I could have started at my new school a Somebody. I would have been a cheerleader.

AUGH!!!!!!!!

So NOW you see why I was soooooo bumming! I just lay in my room. I didn't want to come out. Until Mom came up with the mall idea.

So, OK, whatever. That whole "didn't make cheerleading thing" was this morning. It's so over now. We have better things to think about, right? I am not going to get stuck in the past. I am going to look ahead to the future. And, of course, for some cool, new school stuff at the mall.

So Mom and I drove to the mall and went inside. Mom said she had to pick up a present for Grandma, so if I wanted to, I could go on ahead without her. If I followed safety rules. And didn't talk to strangers. And I stayed right in the area surrounding the food court. And didn't go any farther than there to there to there. And she would meet me at Limited Too in 20 minutes.

Maddy's Back-to-School Shopping List

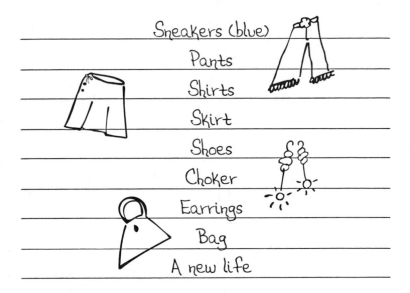

Sneakers (blue)
Pants
Shirts
Skirt
Shoes
Choker
Earrings
Bag
A new life

So there I was at the mall by myself. I walked past the card store, a baby store, and a computer store. I walked through the food court. Should I stop and get a pretzel? A cookie? A smoothie?

It felt kinda weird. It was the first time I'd ever been at the mall by myself. Usually one of my friends would be here with me and I'd be going, "Hey, do you want to stop for a pretzel? A cookie? A smoothie?" And then we'd all decide together. But today I was on my own. Because my friends were all at their first CHEERLEADING PRACTICE.

But really, I'm not obsessing. Really, I'm not.

OK, I am. Because they're all at cheerleading ... without meeeeeeeeeeeeeeeeeeeeeeeeee!!!

OK, I have to stop whining. I am getting pathetic. I did not make cheerleading. Enough already!

GET OVER IT, Maddy!

Oops, did I say that out loud?

I looked around. Yeah, I did say that out loud. This girl with long curly hair walking by with her friends turned around and gave me a look. Like is that girl talking to herself?

Red-face Rating: ☆☆ out of ☆☆☆☆☆ stars. *Talking to yourself out loud: Way embarrassing. Whew, but could have been more stars if more people had heard me.*

The girl with the hair said something and her friends started laughing. Probably about me talking to myself. As Brittany would have said, "Did you SEE that girl over there by herself? She was talking to herself? No wonder she's all alone. What a looooser!" (Oh, and in case you didn't know, here's a heads up. Stay on Brittany's good side.)

I think I'll skip the smoothie and start shopping. I waited til the girl with the hair and her friends had gone around the corner. Brittany wouldn't have been able to say anything nasty about the girl with the hair. That girl looked so totally put together, you couldn't help but notice her. Just her hair alone was amazing. She was wearing great jeans, a tank top, and sandals. I'm sure SHE made cheerleading. She was probably captain. Co-captain, minimum. And she doesn't stand around talking to herself like a crazy girl in the mall.

Great. Now I'm the crazy girl who talks to herself at the mall. I needed to regroup. Put on some lip gloss or something.

I passed a few stores. I remembered there was a girls' room kind of down a hall. There were construction signs all over like a new store was being opened next to it, so I thought it might be closed. Nope, it was open. I pulled the door open and walked past the couch and the chair in the pink waiting room area.

Oh, figures. The girl who had passed me in the mall with her friends was in there at the mirror, fixing her hair. Not that there was anything to fix. Her friends were nowhere in sight.

Look normal, look normal, I told myself. Do not look like a girl who talks out loud to herself.

I went down to the other end of the mirror. I couldn't help but look at her hair. She looked like she should be in a hair commercial.

She noticed me staring at her. Oops, busted.

"I, um, like your hair," I told her honestly, trying to smile like I wasn't staring at her or anything weird.

"Thanks," she smiled back. But she was probably really thinking, "There's that psycho girl who talks to herself! Run for your life!"

The door opened and two other girls came in. I concentrated on my own reflection in the mirror. I put on a little shiny lip gloss and smuched my lips together.

I gave myself a pep talk.

OK, you in the mirror, listen up:

- ☆ Chill out! Get a grip! Get yourself together, girl!
- ☆ Where's your confidence? Find it!
- ★ So what if you're here by yourself? That's OK!
- ☆ You're gonna go get some back-to-school clothes to start a new school year fresh!
- ☆ And have the best school year ever!
- ☆ Yeah, that's right! Cheerleading shmeerleading!
- ★ Look out world! Here comes Maddy!!!

I stuck my lip gloss in my bag, walked past the other girls, and pushed out the restroom door. Or tried to, anyway.

BAM!

Owwwwwww ....

chapter 3

Yes, it's true.

I just walked smack into the girls' room door.

"Are you OK?"

"Are you all right?"

Three girls came running over into the sitting area, looking concerned.

"I'm OK," I said.

I couldn't believe I had just walked into a door. My face was hot and felt bright flaming red. That was totally embarrassing.

"Are you sure you're OK?" a girl with black spiky pigtails asked me. "That was a pretty loud bang. What happened?"

"I was trying to push out the door," I mumbled. "But I guess I was supposed to pull it. Duh." I pulled on the door handle, trying to get out of there fast. My face felt like it was on fire. They probably thought I was the biggest weirdo!

But nothing happened. I pulled on the handle again.

"Here, let me try," said the girl with black pigtails. She pushed, then pulled. Nothing.

"I think it's stuck," she said. "Here, try to help me push."

We both leaned on the door, but it didn't budge.

"Yup, it's jammed," she said.

"I can't believe we're stuck in the bathroom!" said the girl with the pigtails. "I hope this doesn't take forever! You think we're going to be here awhile? Hey, I'm Kacey! With a K! Rhymes with spacey! But I'm not. Ha!"

She said that all in one breath, hopping up and down. That girl had some serious energy. She was really cute, all smiley and bouncy, in her red tee, shorts, and sneakers.

"I'm Isabel," said the girl with the hair I'd seen in the mall. "You think we should bang on the door and let them know we're in here?" She hit the door a couple times. "Helllooooo! Anybody out there?"

I banged on the door, too.

"Potential shoppers inside! You're losing money every second!" I yelled. Kacey and Isabel cracked up.

I peeked at my reflection in the mirror over the pink couch behind me. I was now down to a mild pink. An improvement. But still a dork, after the door in the face.

"So, who are you?" Isabel asked me.

"Um, I'm Maddy," I said. "I must have jammed the door or something. I guess I don't even know my own strength."

I looked over at the other girl who was in there. She was the only one who hadn't said anything. She was just standing there looking at us, but she didn't introduce herself. She did look pretty stuck up. And totally gorgeous. She had long, straight blond hair, blue eyes, and was way taller than me. She was totally prepped out. She sat down on one of the chairs and didn't say anything.

Isabel banged on the door again.

"I guess we just have to wait. I'm sure they'll figure it out soon enough," she said, plopping down on the pink pleather couch.

"Or maybe we're stuck in here for a long time!" I said. "It'll be like a survival show on TV. We'll have to survive on bathroom supplies. At least there's plenty of water," I waved toward the sinks.

"Well, I can contribute to our food supply," Kacey said cheerfully. "I have gum!"

Kacey sat down on the arm of a pink chair and reached into a sports bag.

"Want some?" Kacey asked us. "I've got peppermint and grape. Peppermint's already open, but if you want grape just tell me." She handed the peppermint pack to me. I took a piece and passed it to Isabel. Isabel took one and held out the pack to the other girl, who was still kind of just sitting there on the chair.

"Do you want some gum?" Isabel asked her.

The girl didn't move.

"Hellooo. Gum?" Isabel tried again nicely.

"Maybe she doesn't understand English." Kacey said.

The girl opened her mouth but nothing came out.

I was realizing that she actually wasn't looking stuck-up—more like just stuck. Her eyes were wide open and she was kind of frozen.

"Um, are you OK?" I asked her.

She opened her mouth again.

"Yes. No. I mean, I'm just not very good at being locked up in places," the girl talked almost in a whisper. She didn't really look at us. Her hands were shaking a little bit. "I'm kind of claustrophobic."

"Oh no!" Kacey jumped up. "She's panicking! Is she panicking? Have her lie down! No wait, sit her down! What should we do? Wet towels on her face, maybe? Grab some wet towels!" Kacey ran to the sink and turned on the faucet. She started pulling paper towels out of the towel thingy.

The girl just sat there on the chair.

"Hey, come here, sit on the couch," Isabel told her. Isabel got up and kinda pulled the girl to the couch. She kept talking to her.

"It's OK," Isabel said to her in a quiet voice. "Someone will be here in a minute to get us out. We're just in the girls' room. No big deal. And I know this trick for when you feel panicky. My mom makes my sister do it on airplanes."

I didn't know what to do. I sat on the chair that faced away from them and started going through my bag. So I wasn't staring or anything.

"OK, close your eyes," Isabel was telling the girl. "Now take a deep breath in. Breathe out really, really slowly."

"I feel so stupid," the girl said all quietly, opening her eyes and looking at us. "Sorry."

"Don't feel stupid. Nobody's thinking you're being stupid," Isabel was so calm with her. I was really impressed. I almost had a panic attack just thinking about this girl having a panic attack.

The girl closed her eyes again. She breathed in and out really slowly.

"Now think about someplace that makes you happy and relaxed," Isabel said. "Like I would think of my grandmother's house in the country. What are you thinking of?"

"The horse barn?" the girl said. She closed her eyes.

"Great, think about the horse barn," Isabel said softly.

I thought about my place. It would definitely be the beach, on vacation.

Isabel kept talking to the girl softly. The girl seemed a little calmer.

"You're all right. Everything will be fine," Isabel told her.

OK, OK, OK. I hope this girl is OK.

The girl lifted her head.

"I'm OK," she said in a really quiet voice. "Really, I'm OK."

Whew.

"I'm sorry," she said. "I'm sorry, I just hate being closed in."

"Yeah," I said. "I get that way on elevators sometimes. I only do escalators if I can help it."

"I feel better. Really. I'm Claire," the girl told us. Her

voice was still weak but she looked less scared. "Thanks for helping me."

"Yeah, Isabel. You were great," I told her. Isabel was totally cool under pressure while helping Claire out.

"Oh, puh-lease. It was nothing," she waved it off. She turned to Claire. "Maybe you should lie down and relax."

Claire lay back down on the pink couch.

Kacey was still over at the sinks. She looked at the wet paper towels she had been preparing. There were piles of them filling all of the sinks. One of the sinks was overflowing.

"Oops!" she said, turning off the faucets. "I think I got carried away." We all laughed as she started throwing soggy paper towels in the trash.

I sat down on the chair across from Isabel and Claire.

"This is taking awhile," I said. "Doesn't anyone else in this mall have to go to the bathroom or what?"

"I wasn't sure if this restroom was even open," Kacey called over. "With all the construction signs. But I crashed it anyway."

"I wonder if there's some kind of security phone in this place," said Isabel.

"Oh my gosh!" Claire said, sitting up weakly. "I have a cell phone. We can call security on my phone." She asked me if I would mind getting her flowered bag off the sink. I went over, got it, and gave it to her. She pulled out a purple cell phone, dialed, and started talking.

"Hi, Bruno. It's me." Claire said into the phone, softly. "Yes, I'm still at the mall. Everything's fine. Please don't worry about this at all. I'm just a little stuck in the, uh, bathroom."

A loud man's voice came booming over the phone.

"I'm really fine, Bruno. Please. I told you I can take care of myself today. Can you just report that we're stuck here? First floor, near the bookstore. Yes, I'm fine. Thank you! Goodbye!" Claire hung up. "Bruno's going to call mall security to take care of it," she told us.

"Yeah, Bruno to the rescue," I high-fived Isabel and Kacey.

"Go, Bruno, go!" Kacey cheered.

"Bruno rocks!" Isabel said. "Whoever Bruno is!"

Claire closed her cell phone and lay back down. "Of all the days for this to happen! What are the chances?" she said, almost to herself.

"What do you mean?" Kacey asked her.

"I'm usually not allowed to go to the mall alone," Claire said. "Today they finally said I could. They dropped me off for an hour while my father's girlfriend got her nails done. And now this happens. They're never going to let me out again!"

"Yeah, my parents are like that, too," I told her. "My mom only lets me come here with her or my group of friends—"

Oh no! Mom!

"—And I'm supposed to meet her in, like, five minutes!" I said.

Times my mom has let me shop by myself in the mall before: 0
Times my mom will let me do it again if I don't meet her on time: 0

"Go ahead and use my cell phone," Claire said, sitting back down in the chair. She tossed me the phone. "Call her on her cell."

"She doesn't have one," I said. "And she's going to be really worried if I don't show up."

"Where are you supposed to meet her?" Isabel asked. "Just call the store and tell them to let her know."

"Good idea," I said. I dialed 411 for Information and asked for Limited Too's number.

"Hey, I'm going there, too," said Kacey and Isabel at exactly the same time.

So when the store manager answered, I told her what was going on. She said she'd be on the lookout for a woman with short brown hair, white button-down shirt and khakis named Pam. Who might be rushing around freaked out and calling out my name. And she'd look for Kacey's mom, who was with two girls and who also was really, really pregnant. And to look for Isabel's two friends, who were meeting her there, too.

"OK, we're covered!" Kacey said cheerfully. "Now we wait."

chapter 4

We waited. Isabel put on some lip gloss. Claire closed her eyes. Kacey paced around.

I started cleaning out my bag. I carried a big one. I liked to keep my stuff with me.

- ☆ Lip gloss #1: Clear and very slippery
- ☆ Lip gloss #2: Pink with a teeny bit of sparkle, but not too much
- ☆ Disc player: Dead batteries, bummer
- ☆ Four gel pens: blue, purple, silver, and gold
- ☆ My blue fuzzy journal
- ☆ A friendship slam book
- ☆ The book I was in the middle of reading

"Oh, I just finished that book," Claire said, looking over my shoulder. "I loved it."

"Hey, I read that, too!" Kacey said. "I can't wait for the sequel!"

"You guys like to read? Me too," I told them. "I like to write, too. That's my journal. And that's my slam book." I held it up. "Anyone want to fill it out? I mean, just for something to do."

Isabel took it and opened it up.

"It's blank because I just got it from my aunt. She just sent it to me yesterday as a present, I mean. I didn't have a chance to give it to anyone yet. Not because I don't have any friends!" I babbled on. And blushed.

Now that was a totally stupid thing to say.

"Puh-lease, I didn't figure you for the no-friends type," Isabel said, looking straight at me. Was she being sarcastic because she had seen me talking to myself before like a weirdo? No, she didn't sound sarcastic.

I handed her my purple gel pen. I pulled out my favorite blue one, the one with the glitter, and opened my journal.

This Journal Belongs to:

Maddy Elizabeth Sparks

So this is so totally CRAZY! I am stuck in the girls' room! With 3 girls I don't even know. Total strangers. Not even from my school. We're waiting to be rescued. Those girls are filling out my slam book right now. It seems like this should be a crisis in my NIGHTMARE day, but it's really not so bad. These girls are all totally different. But WAY cool!

☆ **Kacey:** Is like the cutest girl who doesn't stop smiling! But not a fakey smile. Like she's really smiling! Like let's just have fun here! She talks really fast. She has so much energy, like a super bouncer ball or something! She has pigtails and is almost, almost as short as me.

☆ **Isabel:** Ultra-confident. She hasn't whined, complained, or freaked. She's just like soooooo cool. She's a year older than me. She's about medium height, but she seems like she's taller. Maybe she just acts taller! Amazing hair. And the way she puts together her clothes, total Hip Chick. I mean she looks like she should be on a runway somewhere showing the newest trends. You'd think she'd be like majorly stuck-up. But she hasn't been for even one second!

★ **Claire:** I hate her. OK, not really. She is soooo sweet. But if the other two girls are way pretty, she is prettier than even that. She's tall and maybe like a year older than me, too. And classy looking.

What? Oh, they're done with my slam book. gtg. More later.

I opened the slam book and read what everyone had written. First page was mine:

Name: Maddy Sparks
Hair: Brown
Eyes: Green
Family: Mom, Dad, Zack
Pets: Guinea pig, Sugar. I want a dog!!!!!

Sign: Libra
Favorite color: Blue
Favorite food: Pizza with pepperoni and extra cheese
Favorite ice cream flavor: Mint chocolate chip
Favorite sport: Swimming
Hates: Broccoli
Biggest accomplishment: Elected VP of my class last year, winning a ribbon in the Phab Photo contest

Name: Kacey Choe
Hair: Black
Eyes: Brown
Family: My grandmother, my mom, my dad, little sister cutie pie Emily, and mystery baby on the way
Pets: None (Henry the Hermit Crab, RIP)
Sign: Gemini
Favorite color: Red and grey! Like my favorite football team colors!
Favorite food: Chicken
Favorite ice cream flavor: Cookie dough
Favorite sport: Soccer, basketball, lacrosse, diving, track, ice skating, rollerblading, all of them!!!
Hates: Violin!
Biggest accomplishment: Basketball camp prize! Soccer captain this fall!

Name: Isabel Vega
Hair: Brownish black
Eyes: Brown
Family: Mom+Lawrence, Dad+Ana, Jessica, Michael
Pets: Beans, the dog
Sign: Aries
Favorite color: Orange
Favorite food: Pasta
Favorite ice cream flavor: Vanilla
Favorite sport: Track, Jazz, Cheerleading
Hates: People who act fake
Biggest accomplishment: Yet to come!

Name: Claire Fullerton
Hair: Blond
Eyes: Blue
Family: Dad and Harrison and Adam (my stepbrothers)
Pets: Horse, 2 dogs
Sign: Pisces
Favorite color: Pink
Favorite food: Sushi
Favorite ice cream flavor: Black raspberry chip
Favorite sport: Horseback riding
Hates: Being locked up in places!!!
Biggest accomplishment: ?

Kacey was sitting on the arm of Claire's chair. Isabel laid back on the couch and rested her shoes on my lap. Claire handed me the slam book.

"Omigosh, you guys," I said, reading the slam book. "Claire has her own horse!"

"Yeah," she said, shyly. "I've had Skydancer for a year. She's so beautiful."

"Skydancer? That's such a pretty name," Isabel said. "My dog's name isn't so pretty: Beans. Short for Rice and Beans. My brother Michael named him."

"At least you have a dog," I told her. I kept reading. "Kacey, is there any sport you don't play? Your list practically goes off the page!"

"Pretty much, no!" said Kacey giggled. "Well, I've never surfed. Ohio doesn't exactly have the best waves. But that doesn't mean I don't want to try it!"

"I love the beach," I said. "I haven't been in like two years, but I love it. I've never surfed either, though."

"We go to the beach all the time," Claire said. "But I kind of like the mountains better."

"Yeah, so does my little brother. He's into camping and all that. Kacey, you're so lucky to have a little sister," I said. "I have a little brother. He drives me insane."

"My younger sister Emily is really fun," Kacey agreed. "But I might end up with a younger brother, too. My mom is going to have a baby next month!"

"I wish I had a little brother or sister," Claire sighed. "I'm mostly an only child. I have two older stepbrothers, but they're away at school."

"Hey, guess what?" Kacey said. "My mom said that I get to name the baby myself! How cool is that?"

"Maddy's a good name," I said, smiling.

"I'll put it on the list," Kacey said.

Maddy's list of favorite names for the little sister she wants!

- ☆ Courtney
- ★ Miranda
- ☆ Ashley
- ☆ Hannah

"But ugh," said Isabel. "I saw you have to take violin,

Kacey. I went through that torture for a year."

"Yeah, I can't stand it. I can't sit still that long!" Kacey said.

"No kidding!" I burst out.

We cracked up, because Kacey was bouncing all over the place. She hadn't sat down yet!

"Really? You guys don't like violin?" said Claire. "I like it. I take violin and piano."

"I don't take any instruments, but I love music," I said. "At least to listen to."

"Yeah, I noticed your bag!" Isabel pointed to my bag. I had a bunch of pins with my favorite groups on them.

"Oh, I love that group!" Kacey said, pointing to one of them. "That singer is WAY too cute."

Yeah, I thought so, too. He was #3 on my crush list.

Number one was Ryan Moore. He's not a singer or anything. He's a guy in my grade.

With dark brown hair.

Dark blue eyes.

Soooooooo cute.

"Maddy? Earth to Maddy? Hellooooo?"

"Oh, what? Sorry!" I said.

"I just asked you if you want me to do your hair?" Isabel asked me. "Not that there's anything wrong with it. It's just that I like to do hair and I just picked up some new bands."

"Yeah, sure!" I said. She came over and I gave her my comb. She got out some hair bands and started putting my hair up.

"Isabel, I love your hair," Kacey told her.

"It's amazing!" I agreed.

"Thanks, you guys," she said.

"I'm also loving Claire's bracelet," Kacey said.

"This?" Claire said, pulling off one of the beaded bracelets on her arm. She held it out to Kacey. "Here, you can have it."

"Omigosh!" Kacey squealed. "That's not what I meant! I just think it's really cool!"

"Oh, okay. But if you change your mind you can have it," Claire shrugged.

"That was really nice of you, though, to offer it," Kacey said.

"Hey, Claire, I like your shoes," I said.

"Sorry, you can't have my shoes!" she smiled.

"Darn, worth a try," I said.

"Well, what size do you wear?" Claire added. "If you're my size, I can give you these after we get out of here and I get some new ones."

"Claire! I was totally kidding! I'm not taking your shoes," I said.

That girl was way nice.

I shifted around in the chair. We'd been stuck in here for awhile. It was a good thing they had this little lobby area. Otherwise, we'd have to be hanging out in the stalls or something. Gross! I opened the slam book again and scanned Isabel's answers for something. Yup, I was right.

"So, you're a cheerleader?" I said to her. "Do you love it?'

"Hey, I cheerlead, too!" Kacey said. She did a little jump and clap.

"Yeah, it's awesome. I did it last year, too," said Isabel. "Are you a cheerleader?"

Uh, no.

"No. I didn't make the team," I said softly. "I got cut this morning."

"Oh, Maddy," Claire said. "I'm really sorry."

She came over and surprised me by giving me a hug. I can't believe I thought she was stuck-up.

"Yeah, I'm an official loser," I sighed.

Isabel snorted, grabbing my book.

"Some loser. Let's see," she flipped through my book. "It says you were vice president of your class last year. You won a prize for a photo you took ...."

"And you're wearing a cool choker," Kacey interrupted, smiling. "That's really pretty!"

"So, not seeing any loser factor on you, girl," Isabel said, shutting my book and tossing it to me.

"Are you really upset about not making it?" Claire asked. "My school doesn't even have cheerleaders. It's an all-girls school. I don't really think about it. Is it a big deal to you?"

"Yeah," I said. "All my friends made the team. I'm the only one left out!"

"Bummer," said Kacey.

"Yeah, I practiced like all summer, too. I barely went to the pool. I even cut out of camp two weeks early so we could all practice together. And I take gymnastics, I take dance ...." I grumbled.

"So what went wrong?" Isabel asked.

"Um, maybe I'm just not good enough," I answered. "I guess everyone else is just better than me."

"That's not helpful," Isabel said, continuing to put my hair up in bands. "Did you screw up your jumps? Was it the expression on your face? Your coordination? Your spirit? What do you think you need to work on?"

Uh ...

"Did you ask the coach what you could improve on? Did you ask the other girls what they thought?" Isabel continued.

Uh ...

"No, I mean I just figure I stink," I said.

"Don't you want to know for next time? Otherwise how can you work on it for the next time you try out?" Isabel asked. "Do you have any more tryouts this year? Do you have to wait till next year?"

"Well, that was football cheerleading tryouts for the fall," I explained. "There's basketball cheerleading tryouts in September. But you can be on both teams. So I mean, I figure the same girls will try out and make it again. I wasn't going to go through that again. Way too embarrassing. I just don't think I'm cheerleader material."

"That's not very spirited," Isabel shrugged. "For someone who wants to boost school spirit. Rah, rah and all that. I mean, if you REALLY want to be a cheerleader, you should try again. For sure. And get advice now on what you can improve. Maybe you can get another cheer-leader to help you. Or ask a high school cheerleader to help you or something. If you want, I can e-mail you some names of videos and books and stuff I used when I was practicing."

Wow! Did this girl know everything or what?

"Yeah. OK, sure. Yeah," I told her.

"I'll give you my e-mail address," Isabel said. "Toss me a pen—"

KNOCK! KNOCK!

"Ahh!" we all jumped and screamed.

"Hello? Anybody in there? This is the mall manager!" a man's voice yelled through the wall and there was more knocking.

Omigosh! They're here to get us out! I jumped out of my chair.

"OW!"

And sat back down as my hair got yanked. Isabel was still holding on to it.

"Sorry, just putting in the last rubber band," Isabel apologized. "There. You're done."

"Our rescuers have come!" Kacey exclaimed dramatically. "Save us, save us!"

"Stand back, girls," a voice said. "I'm going to work on this door, here ...." We heard some noises like a key in a lock, some banging on the door and then ...

BAM! The door flew open. And two men were standing there in the pink waiting area.

"Door's open," one of them said.

We were free!

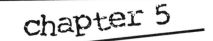

chapter 5

Practically the next thing I knew, I was left alone standing outside the girls' room. It all happened so fast. First, the mall guys broke in to free us. Kacey, Isabel, Claire and I all kind of rushed out of there. Bruno ... who was maybe Claire's father? stepfather? uncle? I don't know ... was there and he rushed her away really fast. The mall manager started talking to me and Isabel and Kacey, saying how sorry he was. And then he gave us each an envelope containing a gift certificate good at any store in the mall. Woo hoo!

And believe it or not, I had to go to the girls' room. I mean, REALLY go. Yes, all that time stuck in the girls' room and NOW I had to go. So I stuck the envelope in my bag and went back in. I double-checked the door to make sure it was working. Did what I had to do really fast. And got out through the door without being stuck this time.

Everybody was gone. The hallway was empty. I was alone.

I felt lonely again, all of a sudden. Not that I wanted to be stuck in the girls' room again, thank you very much. But, when I was stuck in there with Kacey and Isabel and Claire, I'd forgotten about my friends-all-at-cheer-leading-without-Loser-Me situation. I was feeling pretty happy again, like I was hanging out with new friends. But that was weird, right? I mean, it wasn't like I really knew these girls, right? I had only just met them. But I felt like, I don't know, does this sound weird? Like we had some connection or something. I couldn't miss them already, could I?

Omigosh, I never got Isabel's e-mail address. Or anyone else's phone number. Or anything. I guess they'd just be names in my slam book.

Bummer. I didn't even get to say goodbye.

Well, I'd better go find Mom in case she's freaking out. But first, I opened the gift certificate. It was for 50 bucks and I could use it at any store in the mall! Sweeeet! I headed over to meet my mom. I could now go on a serious shopping mission. It was good timing, too. My family had been on a serious budget lately. Now I definitely could get some new sneakers for school. YEAH!

What should I get?

Bright blue?
Light blue?
Dark blue?
Light blue with white?
White with dark blue?

Can you tell I want blue sneakers or what? I am on a blue sneaker mission!

I walked over to the entrance of Limited Too.

"Maddy! Are you OK?!" It was my mom. She came over to me.

"The line at the gift shop was so long, it took me forever to get over here," she said all in this rush. "So I was late. And the store manager told me what happened! I was just about to head down there but they said you were on your way over here."

"I'm totally fine, Mom," I reassured her. "The door just got jammed. I was fine. I wasn't alone. There were three other girls in there. Plus I had gum, lip gloss, and you know, regular bathroom stuff. Everything I needed!"

I saw her look like "Oh my poor baby was trapped!"

"OK, that was supposed to be funny, Mom," I said. She is a major worrier. "Time to celebrate my freedom! Get out of worry mode and into shopping mode!"

"All right, sweetheart, if you say so," she said. And Mom gave me a big huge hug in front of the store.

And we headed into the store, together.

"Hi!" the salesgirl said to us.

"Hi," we said back.

"Ooooh, this is cute!" I told my mom, pulling out a shirt off one of the front racks. "I love the little thingy on it!" She held out her arms and I tossed it to her.

"How about if you wait here and I'll look around?" I asked her.

"Sure, honey," Mom said. "I'll be over there if you need me."

"Maddy!" I heard a voice call out. Kacey came running over. Two girls who were a little younger than us followed her.

"Hiiiiiiii!" we screamed. I even kind of bounced around like Kacey. I was so happy to see her!

"This is my sister Emily and her friend, Storey," Kacey said.

"Hi," Emily said, smiling like a mini-Kacey. She had long straight black hair and was wearing a puppy T-shirt and shorts. Kacey was eating candy from a cell phone-shaped package. Her friend, Storey, had blond hair to her shoulders and was hanging behind Emily, shyly.

"Maddy was one of the girls I told you about," Kacey explained to her.

"Kacey, I found this dress, see?" Emily said, holding up a red dress. Emily even talked like Kacey, all in this excited rush of words. "I love it! But Mom said I don't need another dress. But I have my violin concert coming up. And this would be perfect for it. Can you talk to Mom, pleasepleaseplease?"

Kacey looked at it.

"It is pretty. I'll see what I can do," Kacey told her. "I'll work on Mom for you."

"Work on Mom about what?" a woman came up behind her.

"Oh!" Kacey said. "Hi, Mom!"

Yup, Kacey's mom was really pregnant! She had kind of short black hair and I now knew where Kacey and Emily got that smile.

My mom came over and introduced herself to everyone. The moms started talking to each other. Like, our poor babies trapped in the ladies' room! And all that.

"Pleeeeease don't forget to help me get my dress!" Emily whispered to Kacey. Emily and Storey went over to the makeup table to spritz stuff on themselves.

"Claire, hi! Over here," Kacey yelled out. There was Claire! Over by the dressing rooms!

"Hi!" Claire said. She ran over to us. She was carrying some clothes in her arms.

"Oh, I like that dress," I pointed to a cool one she was carrying. "That would look great on you."

"Thanks, I thought it looked so pretty," Claire answered. "I'm not sure about this one, though." She held up a skirt.

"Uh, no, not so much," I said.

"So not you," Kacey agreed.

Claire put it back on the rack.

"Yeah, that's what I was thinking. But I need a pair of jeans. You guys will have to help me find one," Claire said.

"You seem much better now," I said to her.

"Yes. I mean, not to say I wasn't having fun with you guys but I needed to get out of that room!" Claire answered.

"How cute is this shirt?" Kacey said, holding up one that said "basketball" on it.

"Do they have any shirts that say 'I survived being locked in the bathroom' on them?" I asked.

All of a sudden a pair of hands covered my eyes.

"Guess who?" said a voice.

"Isabel!" we all shrieked. I was so happy to see her!

"Hey, you guys," she said. "What's up! Meet my friends Nicole and Tia."

We all said. "Hi." Nicole had brown hair wrapped up in a spiky ponytail under a visor. Tia had a zillion braids. They were super chic, like Isabel.

"I can't believe you guys were stuck in a bathroom!" Tia said. "Crazy!"

"I was just telling Nicole and Tia what happened to us," Isabel said. "It *is* pretty funny!"

"Remember when Maddy ran into the door?" Kacey laughed. "SLAM! The look on her face!!!"

"Great, thanks for sharing," I said, kidding. "Remember when Kacey filled the sinks with paper towels and they were overflowing?"

We all laughed.

"Remember when Isabel saved Claire?" I said.

"Oh please, I didn't save her. She would have been fine," Isabel said.

"No, you really helped me out," Claire said. "After a while, I even forgot I was claustrophobic!"

We all looked at each other and smiled.

"Hey, Isabel, we're just going to go try on our stuff," Nicole said. "Meet us over by the dressing rooms whenever you want."

"Nice meeting you," Tia said to us.

"Your friends seem nice," I said to Isabel. And then I happened to look out the entrance and see three guys walking by. Brandon Nash, Derek Hogan ...

AND Ryan Moore.

chapter 6

"Hey, I know those guys," I blurted out. "They go to my school."

"Oh yeah?" Isabel took a couple steps toward the front of the store. "Hey, guys that Maddy Sparks knows! Hey!"

Omigosh, omigosh. She's calling them over.

"Wait!" I yelled to Isabel. "Stop, I mean—"

Too late. They were walking back toward Isabel.

Isabel started talking to them. Kacey went over there, too. I tried to hide behind a display.

Yeah, hiding, OK?

"Aren't you going over there?" Claire asked me. "I thought they were your friends."

"Well, I mean I know them from school. Derek, the guy in the blue shirt, I've known forever. Brandon, in the green, not too much. But Ryan, the guy in the plaid shirt, I was in this math extra help class after school with him and um ..." I felt my face get hot.

"Oh, you're crushing on him!" Claire said. She looked over at the entrance. "I see why! He's soooo cute!"

"Maddy! Maddy!" Isabel was waving me over. "There she is, over behind that display!"

OK, I was going to have to go over there. I would just smile and say "hi" to all three of them.

Very friendly like.

Calm, cool, collected.

Yeah, right. It's Ryan Moore!!!!!!

Oh. And I'd have to bring Claire, too. Of course, I couldn't just leave her standing there by herself, could I?

OK, this is going to sound really mean. Because Claire has been like the nicest person in the world today. But she is GORGEOUS. And if I walked over with her, what are the chances Ryan Moore would even notice me?

Exactly. Close to zero. Bad enough pretty-and-so-cool Isabel and sparkly-and-cute Kacey were already over there.

"Um," I stalled.

"Go ahead," Claire said, smiling. "Good luck!" She turned back to a rack and started going through it.

Oh, what the heck.

"Mom!" I called over to Mom, who was near the dressing room. "Derek Hogan and some of his friends are up front. I'm going to go say 'hi,' OK?"

Mom nodded and gestured for me to go ahead.

"Come on over with me," I said to Claire. "I'll introduce you."

We walked over.

"Hi, guys," I said. "This is Claire. Claire, that's Brandon, Derek and um, Ryan."

Yup. Just look at Derek totally stare at Claire.

"Well hi, Claire," said Brandon. "Any friend of Maddy's is a friend of mine."

Oh puh-lease.

"'Sup?" Derek nodded to me. He lived on my street. Our moms are friends. I've known him since like preschool.

I snuck a look at Ryan.

"Hey, Maddy," Ryan said. "How's your summer been going?"

(HE'S TALKING TO ME!!! RYAN MOORE IS TALKING TO ME!!!)

"Gah," I said.

"Good, that's right, it's been good!" Isabel tried to save me.

I nodded.

We stood there.

"Well, it was nice to meet you guys," Isabel said. "But we gotta finish our shopping. See ya!"

"Later," we all said.

"Bye!" I managed.

We all started to walk away. I turned around to get a look at Ryan. He saw me and waved.

"See ya at school," Ryan said.

RYAN MOORE SAID, "SEE YA AT SCHOOL" TO ME!!!!!

I think he said "see ya" to me. I mean, I'm the only one of us at his school. So it had to be me, right?

Did he say "see ya at school" to me?

"Oooh, Ryan said 'See ya at school' to you, Maddy," said Kacey in a teasing voice. "He turned around especially! He's a cutie! What do you think ...?"

"Um, I, barely know him. He was in this math extra help class thing I took," I stammered. But I was smiling. He DID say it! To me!

"Oh, he likes you," Isabel said. "I can tell."

??????!!!!

OK, that was too much for me to handle.

"Um, I think we'd better go shop." My voice came out like a squeak. Yes, shop. Take my mind off of
RYAN MOORE SAYING, "SEE YA AT SCHOOL" TO ME!!!!!
things.

"Maddy and Ryan, sitting in a tree ..." sang Kacey.

"Maddy's face is all red," Isabel teased. "I think she's having a panic attack! Quick Kacey, go get those thousand wet paper towels out of the sinks you clogged up to put on her face!"

"Shut UP, you guys," I said, swatting Isabel with my hand. But I was still smiling.

We went back into the store.

"Oh, I love this song!" Kacey said. She started singing along to the music coming over the speakers as she went to check out some CDs on the racks.

Isabel went to catch up with her friends.

"Hi, sweetie," My mom came over to me. "Did you find anything?"

"Yeah," I said, thinking of Ryan. "Oh yeah, tons of stuff. And clothes, too."

My mom gave me a funny look. She held up a shirt. "Look what I found for you! Isn't this adorable, honey?"

"Um, not me. Let's keep looking." I held up a shirt from

the rack next to me. "Like this one is WAY cool. And this one, too ...."

"Hello, I'm Claire Fullerton," Claire came over to my mom.

"It's nice to meet you, Claire," Mom said. "I take it you're one of the Bathroom Crew?"

"Mooooom, can you not call it the Bathroom Crew? That sounds kind of, you know, icky," I said.

"Girls' Room Gang? Potty Posse?" my mom continued.

"MOM! You're totally humiliating me!" I said.

Isabel and Kacey came over.

"Mom, this is Isabel and Kacey," I said.

"The rest of the Flushing Foursome," Claire said.

"Claire!" I groaned. But I was laughing.

"Here, let me take what you've found so far and get a dressing room," my mom said. I gave her the clothes I'd been collecting and she walked off.

"Hey, Nicole and Tia took off to go to the girls' room," Isabel told us. "I figure I had enough time in there for now, so they're going to meet me back here. I told them I'd send a rescue party if they weren't back in fifteen minutes," Isabel said, holding out a white hoodie with cute designs on it. "Kacey, this would look great on you. Match all your sports pants there." Then she held up a skirt.

"I think this is very Claire," she said. "You could wear it with that necklace over on the top row. And for you, Maddy, hmm, this sweater, with these pants. Would look fab with your new do."

Isabel had put my hair back with all the bands. It did look really cute.

"You have a good eye," the salesgirl said to Isabel as she was passing by. "Those are great choices. Very cool."

"Thanks, I kinda want to be a fashion designer someday. I'm really into it," Isabel said.

"Well, let's see if you're right and this is 'me,'" I said. Aha. I put on the sweater over my shirt and grabbed a pair of sunglasses I'd been eyeing. I pretended I was on the runway and catwalked down the middle of the aisle.

"Modeling the latest styles, it's Miss Maddy Sparks," I announced.

"Wooo hooo!" Kacey, Isabel and Claire started clapping. Other people in the store were looking at us, I know. But I was on a roll. I posed. I blew kisses.

"Go, Maddy!" Kacey cheered. "Work it, girl!"

I gave them my best fake smile. I did my best supermodel moves.

"Whoops!"

Except that one. Those sunglasses were pretty dark. I tripped and grabbed on to the nearest thing. A clothes rack. I fell right into it.

I heard everybody gasp.

Red-face Rating: ✮★★★✮ out of ★★★★★ stars. *Supermodel? No, SuperKlutz.*

chapter 7

Way humiliating. Totally, totally, totally embarrassing. Why was I always like my own personal TV Blooper show???!!!

I had to redeem myself. I pulled myself up off the floor and bowed.

"Ta da!" I announced. "Did anyone catch that on a video camera? Because that could win us big money on America's Most Embarrassing Bloopers!"

Everyone clapped for me, even the salesgirl.

"And to think I thought you were shy," Isabel said after I pulled myself together. Kacey and Claire were over at the wall looking at lamps. Claire was saying she was going to redecorate her room, so they were looking at room stuff.

"Well, sometimes I am, especially at first," I said. Until I get comfortable. And by now I was feeling comfortable with these guys. What could I say?

"Well, I thought you were kind of well, not that nice," I told Isabel. "I mean, I don't now—"

"Really? Why?" she asked me.

"Well, I mean you look all confident and like put together," I said. "But it was really the look you gave me when you first saw me. You know, out in the mall."

"Out in the mall?" she asked me.

"When I was, um, talking to myself." I said. "And you gave me a weird look."

"Huh?" Isabel said. "I kind of remember seeing you on the way in. I was with Nicole and Tia. But, I don't remember you talking to yourself. I definitely didn't give you a weird look. I was probably looking at something else."

"Oh," I said. "I guess I got that wrong."

"Yeah, definitely. You've got a complex, girly!" she said. She reached over to the wall, picked up a big furry pillow and bopped me over the head with it.

"Pillow fight!" squealed Kacey, grabbing another pillow and throwing it at Isabel.

"Hey, hey, guys! Are you going to buy those pillows?" I said in a very serious voice. "Do not mess with the merchandise."

"Party pooper," Kacey laughed.

Claire clobbered me with a pillow.

"And to think I thought you were stuck-up!" I said to her, laughing.

"Oh," Claire got a serious look all of a sudden. "Yeah, people always say that. I hate that. I'm mostly just shy."

"Wait," I said really quickly. I had totally just insulted her. Me and my mouth. "I didn't mean that the way it sounded. Sometimes I say stupid things. I just meant because when I first met you, you didn't say anything. Remember when Isabel offered you some gum? You didn't say anything. So it looked like you were ignoring her."

Plus I thought she was stuck-up because she was so glamorous looking, I thought to myself. But I didn't say that part out loud.

"But really, you were just panicking!" I finished telling her. "So I was totally wrong!" And really, Claire was so ... nice.

Claire picked up the pillows we were playing with. She bopped me over the head with one. And then she put them in a pile. "I love these. I'll buy these for my room.

They'll remind me of you all."

"Hey, so what'd you guys think of me at first?" asked Kacey.

"Bouncy!" I said.

"Fun!" said Claire.

"Happy!" said Isabel.

Kacey smiled. You just couldn't get a bad impression of Kacey. She was too smiley!

"Um, what'd you guys think about me?" I asked, cautiously.

"Well, let's see. My first impression was ... you had a door up your nose ..." Isabel said.

"Oh yeah!" I blushed. "You all thought I was a super klutz! That was your first impression! I haven't done much to change that, I guess."

"Actually, I thought you seemed nice," said Claire shyly.

"And you totally cracked me up," Kacey said.

Awww. Yeah.

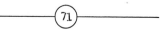

OK, now I felt kinda dumb. I looked around and saw the giant gumball machine.

"I owe you some gum, Kacey," I said, reaching into my bag for some quarters. I went over to the gumball machine. Everyone followed me. I stuck a quarter into the slot.

"I hope it's yellow!" Kacey said. A yellow gumball dropped out of the slot.

"YELLOW!" we all yelled. Kacey did a little happy dance.

"Here's one for Isabel," I stuck my quarter in.

"I wish for ... green," she said, crossing her fingers. Out popped ... green!

"No way! We must be having a lucky day!" she said, popping it in her mouth.

"OK, this is the real test," said Claire. "I wish for ... pink."

I stuck another quarter in. Out popped ...

PURPLE!

We all laughed.

"Well, it kind of has pink flecks in it," she said, looking at it up close.

"That counts," determined Kacey.

"OK, my turn," I said. "I want ... blue!"

I stuck in the quarter and we waited for the gumball to come out the chute.

"Oh, the suspense! Blue, blue, come on blue!" I opened the little door. It was ... orange. I hid it in my hands from the others and stuffed it in my mouth.

"It was blue!" I mumbled, 'cuz my mouth was stuffed with the gumball. "Really, it was!"

"Sure, it was!" Isabel teased me.

"OK, bluish orange, anyway." I smiled. "And that's the story I'm sticking with!"

"No, I totally believe you. Because this is our lucky day!" Kacey said, laughing. And then choking a little.

"Omigosh, I'm going to swallow my gum," she gasped. This cracked us up even more.

"Excuse me, girls?" A lady came over. She had long blond hair tied back in a low ponytail. She was wearing a jacket and long skirt. She looked kind of official. Uh oh. Were we in trouble?

Claire must have thought the same thing.

"I'm buying those pillows, honest," she said.

The woman smiled. "No, that's not what I'm here for. Not that I'm encouraging abuse of our merchandise or anything. I'm Lauren. I work for Limited Too. At headquarters, here in town." She pulled out a card and called one of the salesgirls over.

"Vouch for me, Devon," Lauren said.

"Yup, she's from Headquarters," said the salesgirl.

"I wanted to tell you that I love to see girls having so much fun," Lauren from Headquarters said. "You guys are lucky to be such good friends. Have you been friends for a long time?"

We all looked at each and laughed.

"Oh yeah. At least 45 minutes," Isabel told her.

"Really? That surprises me," Lauren said. "You act like you've known each other for a long time."

"We met under unusual circumstances," I told her. "Called Bathroom Bonding."

"Well, you certainly did click!" Lauren said.

I guess I'm not the only one who felt some kind of connection between us!

"Are you girls here with your parents or an adult?" Lauren continued. "I don't want you to get into trouble talking to me."

One second later Bruno was right in her face.

"Can I help you?" he asked Lauren. She explained that she worked here and showed him her business card. They started talking.

While we waited, Kacey asked Claire if Bruno was her dad or uncle or what.

"Oh, he works for my dad," Claire said. "He drives me around, so I can get places.

"I just have Mom and a minivan," I said.

"Well, my dad's got a lot of business stuff going on so he has Bruno drive me places. It's OK. At least Bruno's pretty nice."

Wow! Claire has a chauffeur! That's pretty fancy. I wonder who her father is! Wait, she told my mom her last name was Fullerton. I was always seeing the name Gregory Fullerton in the newspapers when I was looking for heroic dog stories or ads for free dogs. He was a big-time businessman. Really big time. Hmm?

I saw my mom heading over to us with Kacey's mom. I told her about Lauren. Lauren talked to my mom and Kacey's mom and then my mom told me it was OK to talk to her. And then Lauren waved at some guy to come over. He also looked official.

"This is John," Lauren explained.

We said hi to him and shook his hand.

"John also works at Headquarters," she said. "We've been talking about having a group of girls in for a special project. And after seeing you girls, we're thinking you four are just what we're looking for. I'm going to see if you all can come into the office Monday and we can talk more about it."

??

"What do you mean?" asked Isabel.

"Well, we would start by asking you all questions about our products and things," she explained. "And you'd get to go behind the scenes at Limited Too. And, if all goes well, you'll get to do some very exciting stuff. Very, very exciting stuff! We'll tell you more about it on Monday. Isabel and Claire, we'll have to get permission from a parent or guardian first."

"Wow! Are you serious?" asked Kacey.

"I am. It will be exciting, so I hope you can make it," Lauren said. "It was nice to meet you all. See you again on Monday."

She walked over to my mom and they started talking.

"Omigosh!" I said. "What do you think she meant?"

"I don't know," Claire said. "But I hope my father says yes."

"I'm so psyched," Isabel said. "Just going behind the scenes sounds amazing, whatever that means."

"And did you hear her say 'very, very exciting stuff'?" Kacey asked, jumping all around. "I have goosebumps! Like something big is going to happen!"

Wow.

Could something big really happen to us? To me?

"Hey, you guys!" called out Isabel. She had gone over to the sticker booth. "Come over here! Let's 'sticker' ourselves!"

We ran over to the sticker booth. Claire and Isabel sat on the bottom. Kacey and I squeezed in next.

Isabel put some money in the slot.

"Let's see ...." She selected the sticker that looked like a picture frame with stars on it. We moved our faces around until all four faces looked back at us in the reflection.

One ...

two ...

three ....

"Smile!" Isabel said.

Kacey and Isabel and Claire and I all smiled. Really, really big smiles.

CLICK!

And captured the moment forever.

chapter 8

From: BrittanyCheer
Send to: Haleygrl
CC: Dani55, Shanastar, Jadarox,
           CareBear143, Meggiemegs,
           QuinnQT, Maddyblue
Subject: Cheerleading update!

Hi Cheerleaders! My mom did the schedule for practice so I thought I'd e-mail it to ya! Practice is every Mon, Tues, Wed and Sat till homecoming! And don't forget our Cheerleader Car Wash, Cheerleader Candy Sale, Cheerleaders' Night Out at the Mall, and After the Game Pizza Parties! This will be the BEST YEAR EVER! Gooooo team! XOXOX Brittany

From: BrittanyCheer
Send to: Maddyblue
Subject: RE: Last e-mail

Oopsie! Sorry, Maddy. I didn't mean to CC you on the last e-mail. CYA! Brittany

Ouch.

Last night, after the day at the mall, I was in the best mood. But now, well, back to reality. I was sitting in our family room, checking my e-mail. A mistake. I reread Brittany's e-mail. It looked like I'd never see my friends at school again with that schedule. AUGH!

I deleted Brittany's e-mail.

I felt like the old Maddy. The Maddy-who-couldn't-make-cheerleading-loser-version. Not the Maddy who was at the mall, feeling happy and all excited. Did that Maddy ever really exist?

I leaned back in the swivel chair and put my feet up on the computer desk. Mom would not be happy with me, since I had my sneakers on. But I needed to get a good view of my sneakers right now. Because ...

Those sneakers were my absolute proof that MallMaddy existed! I admired my new blue with white Reeboks. Very niiiiiiice.

And purchased with the $50 gift certificate I got for being stuck in a bathroom. Where I had met Kacey, Isabel, and Claire. And was invited to Limited Too headquarters for exciting adventures ....

About that headquarters thing. Um. I was feeling a little

nervous about it. It seemed so exciting yesterday. Today, every time I thought about it, I felt like I was going to throw up.

I mean, what would I do there? Was there some talent I was supposed to have? Were they going to ask me to do things I didn't know how to do? Was I going to feel all pressured when I was there?

But mostly, would I screw it up? Like cheerleading?

Should I even go? Maybe I should just skip it.

Reasons NOT to go:
- ★ I'll probably screw it up. Totally embarrass myself and all that.
- ★ I'd be wasting their time. Lauren's, John's, the entire company's. They'd figure out I'm not exciting enough to even be there.
- ★ There are a gazillion girls who would be better at it than me. So let one of them have a chance.

Should I go? Should I not go? I needed some kind of sign.

"Ahem," my brother stood at the top of the stairs and cleared his throat. "I'm going to do an imitation for you."

"Zack," I warned. "I am NOT in the mood."

"No, really, take a guess: Who am I?" Zack walked around and then ran SMACK into the wall.

"I'm YOU! Walking into the bathroom door!" Zack laughed hysterically. "Get it? When you trapped yourself in the bathroom!"

AUGH! I put my pillow over my head to drown him out. I soooo should not have told the whole story to Taylor on the phone without double-checking to see whether Zack was listening.

"Now who am I?" I could hear Zack through my pillow ears. Another BAM!

"I'm Maddy getting thrown out of her stupid meeting on Monday. For being a LOOOOOOser!"

"Moooooom!" I yelled. "Zack's bugging me!"

I heard Zack's footsteps retreat. But I could still hear him laughing.

OK, that was it. That was a sure sign I should NOT go on Monday.

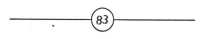

(A sign delivered by Zack? OK, I was pushing it.)

But I just didn't think I should go Monday. I should spare myself the humiliation. If I canceled, I wouldn't have the chance to screw up, right? I could stop being so nervous. And then I could keep the happy memories of the mall. Without any new stupid stuff ruining my memories.

Dling!

The Instant Message bell went off on my computer. It was Taylor's special IM bell! My BFF Taylor was online from Los Angeles, California!

```
TayLA:      Hi! U there?
Maddyblue:  HI!!!!
TayLA:      I M still soooooo excited for
            you!!!! I can't believe what happened
            2 u! u have 2 e-mail me asap after
            Monday!!!
Maddyblue:  Oh. Well, change in plans.
TayLA:      ??
Maddyblue:  Can't go.  O well ...
TayLA:      ?? !!!
Maddyblue:  2 busy. Things 2 do.
TayLA:      MADDY! Tell me the truth.
Maddyblue:  I'm too    :O
TayLA:      Freaked out? y?
Maddyblue:  I'll mess it up.
TayLA:      MAD!!!!! YOU'RE NOT GOING BECAUSE
            YOU'RE SCARED OF SCREWING UP???
TayLA:      MADDY! ANSWER ME!!!
```

TayLA:	MADDY!!!!!
Maddyblue:	Yeah.
TayLA:	U have 2 go. This is the most exciting thing that's ever happened 2U and U just have to go.
Maddyblue:	Seriously, what if I screw it up?
TayLA:	So what? Then yeah u tried. If u skip it u will kick yourself later! I will kick u 2!!!!
Maddyblue:	Good. Come back to Ohio and kick me.
TayLA:	I was going to see if you could visit me this winter here in LA but if u r chickening out about Monday then u will probably chicken out about visiting me.
Maddyblue:	TAY! No, I wouldn't!
TayLA:	Did u tell them yes u were coming?
Maddyblue:	Yeah.
TayLA:	Then you can't break ur word. Just go. Just gooooooooooooooooo! Promise u will go.
Maddyblue:	Maybe ...
TayLA:	Dad's calling. g2g. So pinky swear u will go! Now!
Maddyblue:	K, Pinky swear I will go.
TayLA:	U pinky sweared. U must go. cul8r. Miss u.
Maddyblue:	BFF!!!!!

Oh OKAY. ALL right. I pinky-sweared. I would go on Monday.

I headed to my closet. I guess I'd better think of something to wear.

chapter 9

MADDY ENTERS THE PREMISES

I walked up the sidewalk toward the white Limited Too Headquarters building. Mom was with me. And Zack. (Ugh.) He was walking behind me, stepping on the backs of my shoes.

"Mom, make Zack stop," I turned around and gave him a dirty look. I was soooo nervous. I was still not 100% sure this was a good idea. And Zack was SO not helping.

"Zack ..." my mother said in a warning voice.

"What? What?" He said, all innocent.

We walked farther.

"Hey, is she gonna leave that booger hanging from her nose?" Zack asked.

I ignored him and kept walking. But slower. Did I really have a booger? What, I'm going to believe Zack? I don't think so. But my nose suddenly felt itchy so ...

"I forgot, um, something in the car. I need to run back,"

I said to my mom. She handed me the keys and I quickly ran to the car. I checked my face in the mirror. It was fine. Nothing in my nose. But now that I was checking ... my hair needed help ....

I tried to get my hair to stop flopping in my face. I was wearing one of my new back-to-school skirts, blue of course. I had on a blue and white lightweight sweater and kinda dressy flat shoes. And my lucky choker, of course. Good outfit day.

Not so good hair day. Maybe I should pull it back with a head wrap. I reached into my bag and pulled out a white headwrap.

And then I saw it. A zit on my forehead. OH NO!

"Maddy!" my mom's face appeared at the car window. "Enough procrastinating. We are almost late already."

"Mom, why didn't you tell me that I have a major zit?!!" I asked, pointing to my forehead.

"Honey, we really are running late," Mom said. "You can hardly see it. Come on."

I adjusted my headwrap. (Goal: Cover hair. Also, cover zit.) I walked over to where Zack was waiting.

"Nice zit," he smirked.

I yanked out the headwrap. And did my best to walk and fluff my hair back over my face.

OK. We're at the front door. Here goes.

MADDY ENTERS THE PREMISES, TAKE 2

We were buzzed through the front door of the building.

OK. I could do this. I was invited here. I was not a poser. I was supposed to be here.

We walked up to the front desk, where two people were sitting in front of a bright yellow wall. My mom went over and told them who we were. A woman gave me a tag that said VISITOR on it and told us someone would be right with us.

"Hey, Maddy," Zack whispered. "Just so you know, you don't have any boogers coming out right now."

I waited for his punch line but it didn't come. So I figured that was his way of saying good luck.

"Thanks," I whispered back. "I think."

My mom came over and stood next to us. All of a sudden, I grabbed my mom's hand like I was five or something. She looked down and smiled at me.

"You'll be fine, sweetheart," she said.

WHY AM I SO NERVOUS!!! It's not like they're going to make me perform or anything. Right? I don't think so.

I was inside headquarters! And I really just didn't want to screw this up, you know?

"Maddy!" It was Lauren! Lauren came walking into the lobby and held out her hand. She was wearing her long blond hair in a headband. She was wearing a white shirt, black pants, and some chunky jewelry. She shook my mom's hand, then mine. And said hello to Zack.

"I'm happy to see you, Maddy," Lauren said. "The other girls just went back to the conference room a few minutes ago. I'll take you there."

My mom said she and Zack were going to do some errands and she'd be back to pick me up in a couple hours.

"I'll miss you, Maddy," Zack said, pretending to cry.

I held myself back from sticking out my tongue at him or something equally mature. And instead followed Lauren down a hall. We walked past some offices.

Lauren pointed to an open door. She said she was going to let John know we were all here so we could get started. I could go on in and get settled.

I stopped at the door. All of a sudden I felt that nervous feeling. I hadn't seen Kacey or Isabel or Claire since the mall. Maybe everything would be all weird. Maybe it would be all awkward.

I took one step in. Kacey, Isabel and Claire were sitting at a long rectangular table. Kacey looked up and saw me first.

"Maddy!" she squealed. "Guys, Maddy's here!" She jumped out of her seat and ran over to me. Isabel and Claire followed. They all gave me these huge hugs and ...

I felt a huge smile cross my face.

Yeah.

"We all just got here a couple minutes ago," Isabel said. "Lauren said we would just wait for you and then get started."

"Started on what?" I said.

"We don't know yet," Claire told me. "But I've been thinking about that all weekend!"

Lauren and John walked in.

"Hi, girls," John said. "Have a seat."

We all took a seat. Kacey and I sat on one side. Isabel and Claire sat on the other. John and Lauren each sat on an end.

"Hey, girls, it's really great that you all made it!" Lauren said. "I'll bet you're wondering why you're here. Well, Limited Too really wants your help!

From us? They want our help?

Lauren continued. "Limited Too knows that, since our store is for girls, girls should have a chance to help in making us even better. So, we're putting together a very special group called the Too Crew!"

"And we'd like you four to be our first Too Crew," John said. "That's what we'll be calling you guys. You'll have the opportunity to go behind the scenes at Limited Too. Here are some of the things that you'll be doing ..."

I grabbed my notebook and pen. I didn't want to forget anything he said. So I started taking notes.

☆ We'll get to sneak preview new clothes and other store stuff and give our opinions about them!

☆ We'll go out and talk to other girls to find out what they like and what they're thinking!

☆ We'll get to go to Limited Too events, like concerts and things!

☆ We'll get to meet celebrities!

☆ We'll get to travel to some exciting places!

☆ We'll get money that we can put toward college scholarships. (Aha! No wonder Dad signed my permission form so fast)

"Sound like fun?" Lauren asked.

Ohmigosh. Is she serious?!!!

I looked up from my notebook and around at everyone. They looked totally stunned. It was the first time I'd seen Kacey sit still. Ever.

"Well," John grinned. "Does this sound like something you would like to do?"

Does this sound like something we'd like to do?

DOES THIS SOUND LIKE SOMETHING WE'D LIKE TO DO?!!

We all looked at each other and screamed,

"AHHHHHHH!!!!!!!!!!!!!!!!!!!!!!!!!!!!!!

!!!!!!!!!!!!!!!!!!!!!"

Lauren turned to John and smiled. "I think that would be a yes."

chapter 10

"Good," John said. "Then we might as well get started now. And we're ready to begin with your first assignment. Today's agenda: A catazine shoot. We have a shoot in progress over on the other side of the building. If you'll excuse us for just a moment, Lauren and I will check and see if they're ready for you."

John and Lauren walked out.

I knew the catazine. It's the catalog/magazine I get in the mail. But what would we be doing at a catazine shoot?

"What do you think we're doing at a catazine shoot?" Claire said quietly.

"Maybe taking notes on how things are looking." Kacey guessed. "Maybe just getting an idea of what clothes are coming up or something."

"I can't wait to see the clothes," Isabel said. "Just getting a sneak preview. This is kind of like the first step in my career as a fashion designer."

"Wow, Isabel," I said. "This whole thing is so incredibly

perfect for you. I remember when the salesgirl said you had an eye for fashion. Now you'll be able to really put it to use!"

"Yeah," Isabel said. She was looking seriously happy.

"Ready?" Lauren came back in. "I'll show you the way."

We followed Lauren through a hall, past a coffee bar, to a big room.

"OK, girls," Lauren said. "Today, you are going to be catazine models."

CATAZINE MODELS??? Did she say MODELS?

"You mean we might actually be IN a catazine?" Kacey asked, bouncing from side to side. "Us?"

I looked down at myself. Me? A catalog model? I thought about my Bad Hair Day. And oh no ... my zit! Um, I don't think I'm catalog model material.

"That's right," Lauren said cheerfully. "First, you have to get ready, of course. Here's the game plan ..."

The Game Plan
1. Have a stylist fit us in clothes. (I wonder what I'm going to be wearing?!)
2. Get our makeup done. (But not overdone, Lauren said.)
3. Have our hair done. (Phew! That might—MIGHT— help my bad hair day.)
4. Then, we'll be ready for the photo shoot! (Will I ever be ready for a photo shoot?!)

"Wow," Claire whispered to me. "I feel a little nervous. I always have to get my portrait painted and things at home, but those just hang in my house. Are our pictures really going to be in a catalog seen by millions of people?"

Gee, thanks, Claire. The girl looks like that and SHE'S nervous? What about the rest of us mortals?

Chance I will make it into a catazine

0% ☹ ——————— 100%

Chances IF their makeup people are really, really good.

Ha ha.

This Journal Belongs to:

Maddy Elizabeth Sparks

We're sitting here waiting to start getting ready for our first photo shoot. Whoa. Isabel and Kacey are way excited. Claire and I are way nervous. But I mean, puh-lease. Claire has nothing to worry about. Look at her! I'm practically surprised she hadn't been discovered yet and whisked off to Paris or something to be a supermodel. But me? A model? I just don't have what it takes.

Like a supermodel face like Claire's! Shiny fantastic hair like Isabel's! An amazing smile like Kacey's! I'm just way regular. With my zit. I'll probably be just put in the group scene. Hidden in the back. If they use me at all. AUGH!

Lauren took us to a big room surrounded by offices. She showed us a table with breakfast food on it that we could eat while we were waiting. Bagels, doughnuts, muffins, fruit. There were a couple of women sitting at another long table talking to each other.

"Two other girls are in the middle of shooting right now," Lauren explained. "The women at the table are their mothers. She walked us over to a corner of the room. "And this is Rachel. She'll be doing your hair and makeup."

"Hi! Nice to meet you girls," Rachel said. She had reddish brown hair and was moving makeup and hair stuff around a table. "I'll be just a minute and then we can get started on one of you."

"First we'll get started on wardrobe. We've picked out an outfit for each of you. Let's go meet the stylist and try them on."

We followed her into another room.

Isabel's eyes lit up big time at the scene.

The room was filled with clothes hanging on hooks all over the walls. A long rack held even more clothes. A table in the middle of the room had all kinds of stuff like pillows, stuffed animals, notebooks, and hats. A row of shoes lined the walls.

"I can't wait to be working with all this someday," I heard Isabel say under her breath.

"These are the outfits and accessories for the photo shoot," Lauren explained. "You can see that each outfit has a tag on it so we know what page of the catazine it will be in. Feel free to look around and I'll let the stylist know you're ready for wardrobe."

Lauren left.

"I'm seriously ready for wardrobe," Isabel said. "Check out this outfit right here. These pants and sweater are sweet!"

We all walked around, checking out the different clothes.

"Oooh, I want to wear that!" Kacey said, pointing to a sporty purple outfit. "Love that!"

Two girls about our age came into the room. The blond girl looked really familiar. Where did I know her from ...?

They looked at us.

"Hi, I'm Claire," said Claire. She had the best manners. "And this is Kacey, Isabel, and Maddy."

"Hey," the blond girl said. She was really pretty. But she did not greet us in a very friendly way. "So what agency?"

"What agency? What do you mean?" I asked.

"Talent agency," the brown-haired girl said. "Duh, who represents you for your modeling shoots?"

"We don't have one," Kacey said. "We're all new at this. It's our first time modeling!"

"Oh, amateurs," the blond sniffed. The girl with the brown hair rolled her eyes a little.

Gee, thanks for your support.

"So, you two do a lot of these photo shoots here?" Isabel asked them. She didn't seem intimidated by them.

"Actually no," said the girl with the brown hair. "This is our first time here. But we've done lots of other stuff. Like other catalogs, ads, stuff like that."

"You probably recognize me from my TV commercials," the blond said. "As the Taco Tiko Princess?"

That's it!

"I knew I recognized you!" I said. "You're the girl who goes, 'Mmmm, burritos!'"

"Yes," she said. "But I don't say it like that. I say it professionally."

Ooookay then.

"Oh, I feel a smudge," the blond girl said to the other girl. "Did I smudge?" She tilted her head so the other girl could examine her face.

"No, you look so great, Piper," the girl with the dark brown hair told her. "Your makeup is totally perfect. And your hair, too."

The blond girl gave her a satisfied smile.

Blah. Remind me to avoid these two as much as possible!

"OK, Piper and Sierra," a woman stuck her head in the door. "You're up."

The two girls walked away.

"Bye," said Kacey. "We'll miss you. NOT."

"Oh, just ignore them," Isabel said. "They're insecure." Just then Lauren came back into room with three other women. "This is Toni, our stylist. She has two assistants who will help you get your outfits ready."

"Hi!" we all said. Toni went over to the wall and started pulling down outfits.

"Claire, here's one for you," she said, taking a skirt and sweater and handing it to Claire. Isabel got a cool shirt, jacket, and pants. Kacey got the outfit she had said she wanted.

"Yeah!" Kacey said, doing a little jump. Everyone laughed.

"And Maddy, this one's for you."

My outfit was a sweater, a really cool belt, a choker, and jeans. And my sweater was blue!

"Your favorite color, Maddy!" Claire noticed, too. "That will be so pretty on you!"

"OK, Claire, you're up. We'll get you started with makeup and hair," Toni said. Claire went out the door.

We went out into the main room.

"I'm hungry," Kacey said. "I was so excited I could barely eat breakfast. I need some food."

When we were finished with our clothes, we went over to the food table. Kacey got a doughnut, Isabel took a muffin and I took a bagel.

We sat down to eat.

"I was too nervous to eat breakfast," I said to Isabel and Kacey. "Actually, I was so nervous this weekend, I almost didn't come today."

"Are you serious?" Kacey said. "I never in a million years wouldn't come. I was counting the minutes."

"I'm glad you came," Isabel said. "It wouldn't have been the same without you, Mad."

"OK, Maddy, you're next!" Rachel called out.

Rachel had me stand up in front of a long mirror. She had a ton of makeup, brushes and hair stuff laid out in front of me. I had never had my makeup done for me before. Actually I didn't wear any makeup besides my lip gloss. I wondered what colors she would put on me.

Bright blues!
Bright pinks!
Greens!
Purples!

"I'm thinking a light brown for your eyes and a pale pink gloss on your lips," Rachel told me. "We have to put extra makeup on, otherwise the bright lighting on the set will eat it up. We put on more than you'd usually wear. But we don't want to overdo it. We want you to look natural."

Or
Light brown!
Pale pink!

"Just relax your face," Rachel said.

I tried to relax my face. I felt a little squinty, but Rachel didn't seem to mind.

She put some concealer around my eyes. When she pulled my hair back I cringed.

"I have a zit," I confessed. I hoped she wouldn't toss me out of there.

"Honey, at your age, who doesn't?" Rachel said, unconcerned.

Whew.

Rachel dabbed cover up around my eyes and on parts of my face. She darkened my eyebrows, which she said would frame my face. She dusted powder on me, so it wouldn't look shiny under the lights. Then, eye shadow and mascara. The mascara was the hardest part because I kept blinking. She used a little brush to put on some lip stuff. And then ...

"OK, you're set."

I looked at myself in the mirror.

"Hey," I said softly. "You made my eyes look really pretty!" I did look pretty good. Mostly like myself, nothing major changed. But a little shinier, sparklier, prettier.

"And my zit is gone!" I burst out.

"Ah, the wonders of concealer," Rachel smiled. "You look great."

I smiled at my reflection.

"Thanks, Rachel," I said.

"Now go have fun," Rachel said.

I hopped off the chair. Rachel called Isabel over. I went back to the table. Kacey was talking to a girl I hadn't seen before. She had blondish-brown hair, with some braids pulling back her bangs.

"This is Maddy!" Kacey introduced me. "And this is Alexa. She's a model for the shoot, too."

"Hi," Alexa said. She seemed way more friendly than that Piper and Sierra.

"I really like your makeup," Alexa said to me. "You have pretty eyes."

"Um, really?" I said. That was nice!

"Alexa is doing this shoot and then going to LA tomorrow. She's auditioning for some stuff like TV shows out there," Kacey told me.

"My very best friend in the world lives in LA!" I told her. "That's so cool you're doing that."

"Yeah, I'm really excited about it. I almost can't believe it!" Alexa said. We heard someone call out her name.

"Oops, gotta go. I'm supposed to go get my outfits now. That's my favorite part, trying on all the clothes! But

maybe we can talk more later, you guys. See ya!"
She headed toward the wardrobe room.

"She seemed really nice," I said.

"Yeah, she was," Kacey said.

We didn't say it, but I knew we were thinking: Unlike Piper and Sierra!

chapter 11

"Ready for your new hairstyle?" Rachel said to me. I was back at her makeup area. Now it was time to get my hair done.

"I couldn't exactly get it to do anything right," I told her. "My hair is sort of floppy today."

Actually, every day.

"Not a problem," said Rachel. First, she brushed. Then she took out a flattening iron and ran it through my hair. Then she took out some little brown butterfly clips. She twisted sections of my hair around her fingers and stuck the clips in. She used mousse to make the ends all spiky and then sprayed on some hair spray.

"There you go," she said. I looked in the mirror.

COOL!

"Thank you!" I said and hopped off the chair. I was glad I was getting my picture taken today. Because I looked goooooooood.

I mean, for me.

I went into the wardrobe room. I put on the outfit they had chosen for me. For me! And it was a good choice! Because

I LOVED IT!!!

When I was ready, I walked out into the main area. Isabel looked ready, too.

"Wow, Isabel! You look great!" I told her. Her curly hair was down, long and flowing. "You have such amazing hair."

"Thanks! You, too. Your hair looks great," she told me.

"Well, Rachel's really good then, I guess, to make my hair look good," I said. "Because my hair is always just kind of hanging there. I am a walking bad hair day. I wish I had hair like yours —"

"Hey, Maddy," Isabel interrupted. "Can I give you some advice? When you get a compliment, just say, 'thanks.'"

"Oh," I said. "Yeah. I don't take compliments too well." I wasn't very good when somebody said something nice about me. I always felt dumb.

"Hey, guys!" Kacey ran over. "Maddy! Your hair looks great!"

"Um. Thanks." I said.

Isabel gave me a smile.

"I love yours, too," I told Kacey. They'd put Kacey in pigtails, and they were spikier and cuter than ever.

"Yeah! Check these out! These are the best pigtails I ever had!" Kacey twirled around.

Claire walked over.

"Wow, Claire. You look amazing!" Kacey said.

She did, of course. Her long blond hair was hanging down, all light and floaty around her face.

Claire gave a shy smile. I don't think she was so good at taking compliments, either. I'm sure she got them all the time, too!

So, I would never look like that. But I'd been fussed over, fluffed up, and made up. I felt ...

Good.

Yup. I was actually feeling, really good about myself.

Suddenly, Piper and Sierra came back in the room from their shoot.

"That was so awesome," Piper said loudly.

"Yeah, we rock," Sierra agreed. They walked over to me.

Piper looked me up and down.

"So, when are you going in for makeup and hair?" she asked me, all snotty.

"Yeah, when are you going to get ready?" Sierra echoed.

They both laughed.

My face turned bright red.

Piper was still cracking up as she walked to the other side of the room. Sierra followed her.

I knew what they were doing. I knew they were just trying to get to me. But I couldn't help it. I just didn't feel ... as good anymore.

I went over and looked in the mirror. Who was I trying to kid? I just didn't belong here. Piper and Sierra knew it. I knew it. And pretty soon everybody else would see it, too.

"OK, Maddy," Lauren stuck her head in the room. "Everybody's heading into the other room for the shoot. Follow me!"

I followed her down the hall. I walked in.

"Lauren said we could watch for a minute and see how it works," Kacey whispered. "Isn't the set cool?"

The set was a bunch of tall white and black curtains that closed off an area to make a little room. There were lights everywhere. Music was cranked up on a radio. A bunch of people were moving around, setting things up.

Lauren came over and stood next to me.

"Who are all those people?" I asked her. This is what she told me:

- ★ The producer who makes sure everything about the catalog works from start to finish
- ★ The creative director who creates the look and feel of the photo shoot
- ★ The merchandising people who make sure the stuff in the catalog represents what's going to be in the stores
- ★ The stylist and her assistants who dress the models and make sure they look right on camera

★ The photographer who takes the pictures and his two assistants

And, the models of course! Like me! And Kacey and Isabel and Claire!!!

"Hi," the photographer came out to introduce himself. "I'm Ron."

We all said, "Hi."

"Next up, the girl in the white and the girl in the purple," Ron called out to the other side of the room.

That was Piper and Sierra. They went up to the set. Piper tossed her hair back and gave Ron a big smile.

"That's the first time I've seen that girl smile," Kacey said. "I wonder if she ever does it off-camera."

Ron got his shot ready. Piper and Sierra moved around the way he told them.

"I have to admit it, those girls know what they're doing," Isabel whispered. I nodded. They were good. They seemed all relaxed and natural.

"They don't even look nervous," I whispered.

"Wish I could say that about me," Claire whispered back. "I'm a nervous wreck."

"Well, you don't look it," Isabel reassured her. "Let's just go up there and have fun."

"Great job," Ron told them.

Piper's smile disappeared the instant she was off the set. She and Sierra came our way.

"Did you hear him say great job?" Piper said loud enough for us to hear. "I bet that was the cover shot."

"Ooh!" Sierra squealed. They walked away.

"OK, time for the quad!" the creative director announced.

"That means you four girls come on up!" the stylist gestured toward us.

WE WERE UP! IT WAS OUR TURN!

!!!!!

I followed Kacey, Isabel, and Claire up to the set. The lights were bright. It felt hot up there. I hoped I wouldn't get all sweaty. I started to feel nervous.

The photographer, Ron, told me to stand at one end, then Kacey, then Isabel, and Claire. He told us to put our arms around each other's shoulders and get real close.

"First we need to check the lights," one of his assistants said. "We use this light meter."

He held out a little metal thing and waved it over each of us.

"Light's good," he said.

"OK, we're going to have some fun here," Ron said. "This one's just going to be you girls hanging out, having fun."

Rachel came up and started putting more powder on our faces. She fixed my hair a little bit.

"Maddy, relax your arm," Ron said.

I tried to relax my arm around Kacey.

"Give me a big smile, girls. There you go," Ron said.

I gave what I hoped was a good smile. I felt like there was a big light in my face, though.

"Maddy, I know it's bright, just try not to squint," Ron said.

I widened my eyes.

"Lean in closer, girls!" Ron said. "Closer, closer .... Great smile, Kacey, good Isabel, keep it up. OK, Maddy. Be alive! Be animated! That's better ...."

Ron took an instant-film picture and he passed it around to the other people working. I guess that was like a test shot.

"Looks good. OK, now we're going to pump it up. Turn up the music, please! There you go, girls. Kacey, great smile! Isabel, looking good. Claire, Maddy ... Very nice! ..."

The flash started going off as he took pictures.

"Party mood here, alright!" Ron said. The music was cranked up and the crew started kind of dancing around the set. Woo-hoo! Whoo!

Party mood, party mood! Yeah!

"OK, we're getting into it!" Ron said.

Alright! I was getting into it!

"Work it, girls!" Ron called out.

OH YEAH, OH YEAH, I WAS WORKING IT!

"Maddy, relax, you're just a little stiff," Ron said.

Or, maybe not.

"Maddy, lean in just a little closer ..."

Ooook, I leaned in a little closer. Big smile, big smile, don't squint, don't squint, relax, relax, party mood, party mood ...

And then I heard Piper's whisper carry across the room.

"Maddy, Maddy," she imitated Ron's voice. "Stop ruining the shoot!"

I heard Sierra cracking up. I felt like such an idiot. I tried to lean in even closer, and leaned into Kacey.

I guess I leaned too hard into Kacey. Because I fell over into Kacey. Make that, on to Kacey.

"Oops!" Kacey said. She started to fall and grabbed on to Isabel. Isabel went over. And dragged Claire down with her. And I landed on top of all of them.

Ohmigosh. Ohmigosh.

Red-face Rating:

☆☆☆☆☆☆☆☆☆☆ out of ☆☆☆☆☆ stars.

Off the charts. And off the photo shoot.

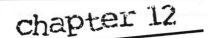
So we were all lying on the ground in this pile. I shut my eyes so I could pretend this wasn't happening. And to hold back my tears.

"And the grand prize winner of America's Most Embarrassing Bloopers is ..." Isabel said loudly. "The Bathroom Crew!"

Then Claire started to crack up. Kacey giggled. I looked in the mirror and saw a big pile of girls. Us.

I couldn't help it. I burst out laughing, too.

We just lay there in a heap, laughing, and laughing.

"Ow, stop, my sides hurt," Kacey gasped. We all cracked up again. Finally, we started to get up. Isabel grabbed my hand and pulled me up.

"OK, CUT!" Ron called out.

I looked out at Ron. All of a sudden, the smile disappeared from my face. I realized what I had done.

I screwed up again. I really did screw up the photo shoot.

And it wasn't funny. Ron was saying something to me, but I couldn't listen. I just ran to the back of the room. I didn't look at Piper and Sierra. I was sure they were totally laughing at me. I didn't blame them.

I am such a LOSER!
I screw up EVERYTHING!
I knew I never should have come.

I leaned against a wall. I was really trying not to cry. Stupid, stupid. That was so stupid.

And then Lauren appeared and stood next to me.

"Maddy, I brought you a bottle of water," she said.

"Thanks," I said, quietly.

"I hope you've been enjoying your time here today," Lauren said.

I tried to sound cheerful. I mean, she was probably feeling bad enough she picked me to do this in the first place.

"Um, it's been really great to see everything," I told her. "Now when I get my catazine I'll be like, I was there!"

"It's fun having you girls be a part of it," Lauren said.

"Thanks for just letting me come today," I said and I meant it. "But seriously, don't worry about me. This is way more than I expected to happen. I'm OK."

"I'm not sure what you're getting at, Maddy," Lauren looked puzzled. I looked down and picked invisible fuzzies off my pants. I took a deep breath and explained.

"I know you were just choosing me because I was part of the stuck-in-the-bathroom group," I explained. "I know I'm not gorgeous and glamorous like Claire. I'm not all bouncy and adorable and cheery like Kacey. I am not this hip trendy girl like Isabel. It's really OK, I know the deal."

Lauren gave me this looooong look.

"Maddy, you've got it all wrong."

Huh?

"You were actually the first girl in the store we noticed. Remember when you fell and jumped up and said you could make money on a TV blooper show? Some girls would have run away if that happened to them. But you just jumped up and recovered and made everyone laugh. That really impressed me."

Lauren took a sip of her coffee. "This morning before you got here, Kacey, Isabel, and Claire had some nice things to say about you."

"They did?"

"Oh yes. Kacey talked about how funny you were. Isabel brought up how smart you were. And Claire said that you were the kind of person she could relax and be herself around. And I get the feeling Claire doesn't have many people she can be that way around."

"Yeah, because I make everyone else look good, probably. Because I do such dumb things," I mumbled. "Face it, I'm just not Too Crew material."

"Maddy, is that what you think we want? Girls who are perfect? I personally think that would be pretty boring," Lauren said. "I'll tell you my description of a Too Crew girl: Smart, compassionate, willing to try new things, with a good sense of humor ... all of those qualities that describe YOU, Maddy."

Oh.

Wow.

I looked at Kacey, Isabel, and Claire hanging out with

the photographer. They were so awesome. It was hard to stay too bummed around those guys. Kacey always cheering you up. Isabel always saying something to make you think. Claire might not say much, but she would listen and give you a hug.

"So, Maddy, you are a Too Crew girl. And, you're about to be a Limited Too catazine model," Lauren continued, snapping me out of my thoughts.

"Maddy! Come on," I heard Kacey's voice.

"Are you turning diva on us, girl? Get over here!" Isabel yelled.

I pulled myself together and went over to see what was going on. Piper and Sierra did, too. The creative director was holding up an instant photo.

"I think this could be our catazine cover, girls," he said. "Take a look."

"It's awesome!" Kacey squealed.

I skooched between Isabel and Claire to see. And I gasped. It was a picture of the moment just after I knocked everyone over. Kacey, Isabel, and Claire and I were kind of a jumble on the floor. We were laughing and

I had a silly grin on my face.

"But, um, that was after I knocked everyone over!" I blurted out.

"Exactly! It's so real! The laughter! The smiles!" Ron said. "It screams fun and friends! It's real and happy! It's perfect!"

!!!!!!!!!!!!!!

"So great job, girls!" the creative director said. "That's a wrap!"

High-fives all around! People were clapping! Kacey, Isabel, Claire, and I were jumping up and down!

Woo-hoo! We did it! We did it!

We including ... ME!

!!!!!!!!!!!!!!!!!!!!!!!!!!

Then I heard Piper's voice from around the corner, all ticked off. "How come they get to be the cover shot?! Don't these people know that I'm the Taco Tiko Princess?!!"

Kacey, Isabel, Claire and I looked at each other. And totally cracked up. And I couldn't stop.

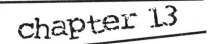

chapter 13

Kacey, Isabel, Claire and I sat in the conference room. The makeup was scrubbed off. We had our regular clothes back on. Our hair was still done from the shoot, though. Isabel was examining Kacey's pigtails.

"That's pretty cool how she did that loop thing with the bands," Isabel murmured. "I'm going to have to practice that one."

"Ladies!" John walked in. "Congratulations on a successful photo shoot."

We all smiled.

Lauren walked in behind him. "We hope you all enjoyed your first assignment. It will be exciting to see the results in the catazine!"

"And we'd like to thank you for your hard work today ... with a little gift," John said.

He took out four little boxes and passed them to Lauren. Lauren spoke.

"We're giving each of you a charm bracelet. I hope it is

a wonderful reminder of the day you were stuck in the girls' room and first became the Too Crew. With each assignment, we'll add a new charm to your bracelet so you can have a memento of every Too Crew experience."

Lauren handed Kacey a box. "Kacey, this is for you."

Kacey opened her box and took out her charm bracelet. It had one charm dangling from it.

"Your charm is a soccer ball," Lauren said. "And not just because you play sports. It represents your bouncy and cheerful personality. You bring everyone up when they're feeling down."

"Thanks! I love it!" Kacey said. "Look, you guys!" She held out her bracelet so we all could see it. She had a big smile on her face, even bigger than usual, if that was possible.

"Isabel, here is yours," Lauren handed Isabel a box. Isabel opened it and held up her bracelet so we could see it. It had a charm of sunglasses.

"The sunglasses represent how you stayed cool under pressure when you were in the ladies' room. I've heard the story how you helped Claire and how reassuring you were. Your confidence helps bring strength to everyone around you."

"Thank you," Isabel said. She put her bracelet on her wrist.

"Claire," Lauren handed Claire a box. Claire took out a bracelet with a cell phone on it.

"The other girls told me how you helped everyone get out of the ladies' room by using your cell phone. But they also told me how you shared your cell phone with them and have continued sharing ever since. This charm represents your generosity."

"Thank you," Claire whispered, with a sweet smile on her face.

"And last but not least, Maddy." Lauren handed the final box to me. My hands were a little shaky as I opened it. I pulled out my charm bracelet. The charm dangling from it was a little sparkly glass slipper.

"Oh, it's so pretty," I breathed.

I thought about how I had thought the day I didn't make cheerleading was the worst day of my life. How nothing was going right. And how miserable I was. And then I got stuck in a bathroom, which should have added to the misery.

And instead, it turned out to be the best day of my life.

"Maddy, I wanted you to have the glass slipper charm," Lauren said. "So you always remember that dreams really can come true."

Lauren fastened my charm bracelet on my wrist for me.

I looked around at Kacey, Isabel, and Claire. They were all smiling at me. I thought about all the exciting things that had happened to us already. And the many more exciting things that were coming.

And then I couldn't hold back.

"Um, can I say something?" I asked Lauren.

"Of course, Maddy. Go ahead."

I took a deep breath.

"This sounds kinda dumb, but the day we met I felt like we had some kind of connection," I said. "And I just want you guys to know I'm so glad I met you. Every time I wear my bracelet I will think of each of you. And of all of us together. These bracelets will link us together, forever." I held my arm with the charm bracelet out and put it in the middle of the table.

Isabel put her hand out on the table, too. Then Kacey, then Claire. Our charm bracelets touched as they sparkled in the light.

Happy Face Rating:

out of

the end ... for now that is!

check this out
and get "tuned in" on what's happening next!

Sneak Preview of

EPISODE #2

Hey!

It's me, Maddy Sparks! Can you believe all of this has really happened to me? Well, wait til you see what's happening next!!!

Right this very second, I'm sitting on an airplane. And guess where this plane is heading ...

HOLLYWOOD! Oh yeah, Hollywood, California. Like, where TV shows are filmed. Where TV shows with famous TV stars starring in them are filmed. Like where TV shows with famous TV stars in them are filmed that I get to go watch happen.

Yes, me! Maddy Elizabeth Sparks! Flying off to watch a television show being filmed and to meet some TV stars!

Is this a normal thing that always happens to me? Because I'm so glamorous? Oh puh-lease. I have never done anything exciting in my entire life ... up until like 10 days ago. That's right, it was just 10 days ago when I was all bummed out because I didn't make cheerleading ... and I ended up a Limited Too catazine model!!!

!!!!

And ...
It just keeps getting cooler!
Even more exciting!!
Even more awesome!!!

Because now I'm off to Hollywood to help out with a contest, where the winner gets to go behind the scenes of a TV show. And not just the winner, but—ME! And in the airplane seat next to me is ... Kacey! And across the aisle ... Isabel! And ... Claire!

We're going to the land of the stars!!!!!!!!!!!!!!!!!!!!

AHHHHHHHHHHHHHHHHH! I CAN'T WAIT!!!!!!

Stay tuned ... and get TUNED IN'

Get the inside scoop at www.LimitedToo.com

the
too crew's
stuff for
you to do

Get CHARMed
(A BRACELET THAT IS!)

It's your turn to pick a charm for YOUR charm bracelet! Which one would you put on your bracelet first?

A soccer ball like Kacey?

Sunglasses like Isabel?

A cell phone like Claire?

A glass slipper like Maddy?

Or something unique for you?

Write YOUR first charm, here:

_____

_____

Other cool charm ideas here:

_____

_____

_____

Q&A with Maddy

Really? You have "Q's" for me? I don't know if I can "A" them but I'll try ...

Q: Dear Maddy: I totally do embarrassing things, too! I trip, spill things, say dumb stuff. How do you deal with it?

Signed, Embarrassing Elana

A: If I were a real regular Advice Columnist I would probably say: "Embarrassing things happen to everyone. So don't be embarrassed!"

But how not true is that? Every time something embarrassing happens to me I feel embarrassed. Humiliated! Mortified! Red-face ratings up to a zillion!

But since I've had a lot of practice, I guess I do deal pretty well. That's what Lauren told me, anyway. So have a look on the next page to see what I do!

STEP 1.
Laugh. OK, you have to laugh at yourself. 'Cuz if you do something embarrassing, then most likely everyone is going to be laughing AT you. Especially the Pipers and Sierras of the world. Ugh. But if you're laughing too, then they're laughing WITH you instead. Get it?

STEP 2.
Don't go all crazy about it. You don't want to overreact. Like cry or run away. Then people will be thinking, wow, she really screwed up. Look how crazy she is being. And they'll feel sorry for you and talk behind your back. So you have to stay cool about it.

STEP 3.
Get over it. Say something about it once. Like "Can you believe I did that? That was too funny." And then, don't bring it up anymore. If you get over it, other people will, too.

Hey!
Sign my Friendship Slam Book!

Name:_____

Hair:_____

Eyes:_____

Family:_____

Pets:_____

Sign:_____

Fave color:_____

Fave food:_____

Fave ice cream flavor:_____

Fave sport:_____

Hates:_____

Biggest accomplishment:_____

There's a copy that your bff can fill out on the next page!

Have your BFF fill-out this page

Name:_____

Hair:_____

Eyes:_____

Family:_____

Pets:_____

Sign:_____

Fave color:_____

Fave food:_____

Fave ice cream flavor:_____

Fave sport:_____

Hates:_____

Biggest accomplishment:_____

pop quiz!

Which "Too Crew" style are you?

Circle the answer that best describes you:

1. You have a free afternoon. You would choose to:

    a) Go rollerblading or shoot baskets
    b) Go shopping
    c) Ride your horse or write poetry
    d) Call your friends and hang

2. Your fave color is:

    a) Red
    b) Orange
    c) Pink
    d) Blue

3. Your closet is mostly full of:

    a) Sport shorts and sneakers
    b) Funky trends
    c) Pretty skirts and dresses
    d) Jeans and tees

Answers:

Mostly A's: You're most like Kacey! Sporty, energetic and always on the go!

Mostly B's: You're an Isabel. Savvy, hip and up-to-the minute style!

Mostly C's: You're a lot like Claire. Cool and classic!

Mostly D's: Mostly Maddy! You have a casual comfortable style!

Combo: You have a style all your own! Mix & match!

This Journal Belongs to:

Maddy Elizabeth Sparks

☆ ☆

☆ Ok ... bye ... this is the end! But not really! Did you read that sneak preview yet? (BIG hint -- I can't wait to go to Hollywood!!!!!!)

You'll find out what happens next to me, Kacey, Isabel, and Claire in

TUNED IN: Episode 2!!!!!

Coming soon exclusively to Limited TOO!

♡Love,
Maddy

p.s. check out more stuff about us at limitedtoo.com